My Princess Collection

Jessie

A Rootin'- Tootin' Cowgirl

Book Five

BASED ON THE Disney · PIXAR FILM *TOY STORY 2*

Written by M.L. Dunham

For information address Disney Press, 114 Fifth Avenue,
New York, New York 10011-5690.
First Edition
Printed in China
9 10 8
ISBN 0-7868-4598-8

For more Disney Press fun,
visit www.disneybooks.com

Chapter One

Hey, howdy! My name's Jessie, and I'm the yodeling cowgirl. *Yooo-de-lay-hee-hoooo!* How about that?

Well, I could yodel for hours, but I'm really here to tell you the story of my pal Woody. He's the rootin'-est, tootin'-est sheriff in the wild, wild West.

You see, a little while back, Woody and I were in this popular TV series called *Woody's Roundup*. Woody was the star, of course, being a brave sheriff and all. Woody's trusty steed, Bullseye, and the Prospector were there, too.

Anyway, our story begins just a little while after that little while back. You see, some of us had been made into popular toys that kids could play with while they watched the show. Over time, the show got cancelled, and toys like us became kind of valuable.

That's when this toy collector fellow named Al McWhiggin came into the picture. He collected me, Bullseye, and the Prospector. But he was missing a big part of his collection: he needed an authentic Woody doll in order to sell the whole set of us for a lot of money.

So, Al toynapped Woody from his home
where he was living happily with this kid
named Andy. That was when the real adven-
ture began. . . .

Chapter Two

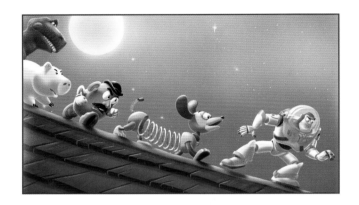

William hat Al didn't realize was that Woody had a whole room full of loyal friends who would do anything to save him. Buzz Lightyear took the lead on the rescue mission. He was Woody's best friend.

"Woody once risked his life to save me," Buzz said. "I couldn't call myself his friend if I didn't do the same." So that's what he did: he set out to save his pal . . . joined by a few other of Woody's toy buddies.

Anyway, Woody ended up with me, Bullseye, and the Prospector over at Al's apartment. You wouldn't believe Woody's reaction when he first saw us. We all ran out to greet him and acted as if we had known him forever (which we had), but he got all confused.

"Okay, I'm officially freaked out now," he said, looking at us like we were strangers. See, he had never even known that he had starred in his own TV show.

Finally, the Prospector spoke up and said, "You don't know who you are, do you?"

Well, we showed him a few old episodes of
Woody's Roundup, and then we let him see all
the toys and things that had been made for
his TV show. He couldn't believe it! When he
saw his picture all over the place, he just
about did a flip.

Chapter Three

'Course, we were pleased as punch that Woody had joined us. Al even brought in the best toy cleaner in town to spiff him up.

With the addition of Woody, it now meant we could go live in a museum in Japan. We would never have to worry about being outgrown by some kid who decided we were no longer fun.

Okay, I have to admit here that I once belonged to a girl myself. She was the best. Then one day, she just grew up and didn't want to play with me anymore. Next thing I knew, I was put in a giveaway box. It nearly broke my heart.

So, you can understand how living in a museum seemed much safer to me. What we didn't realize was that Woody's pals were on their way to rescue him!

We almost had Woody convinced that
going to the museum was better than trying to
get back to his kid, Andy. Then, go figure, all
his toy pals from Andy's room showed up to
save him!

"We're here to spring you, Woody!" cried
his friend Slinky Dog.

Chapter Four

But Woody didn't want to leave us. "They need me to get into the museum," he said.

His friends were sad as they left Al's apartment without Woody.

Then Woody looked up at the TV and saw a kid who looked just like Andy.

Well, after seeing that, Woody decided to go back to Andy, after all. But I have to say, that fella Woody has some loyalty. He decided to take us with him. He wanted us to see that toys are meant to be played with and loved by kids, not sit on a stuffy museum shelf.

Woody called after his pals, but it was too late. The Prospector stood in Woody's way. The Prospector had never been loved by a kid before, and he didn't want to be. He wanted to stay all neat and clean in a museum.

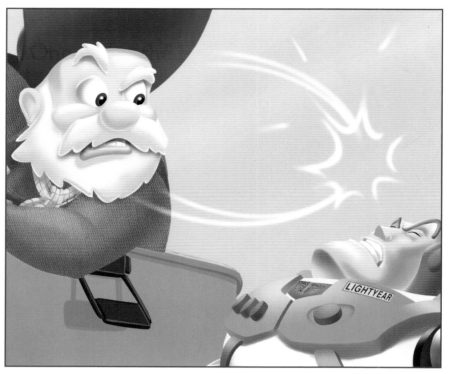

Then—you'll never believe this—Al came home. He packed up Woody, Bullseye, the Prospector and me and headed for the airport. We were on our way to the museum in Japan.

Well, Woody's pals just wouldn't give up. They followed us all the way to the airport. They freed Woody and Bullseye. The Prospector was fighting mad.

But good ol' Buzz and Woody worked as a team and took care of him. They put the Prospector in a little girl's backpack and sent him away forever.

Then Woody, Buzz, and Bullseye did a real rootin'-tootin' rescue . . . of me! They actually galloped all the way out to the airplane, where I had been loaded in the cargo hold.

I thought I was done for. But those crazy fellas actually got me out of the airplane just as it was about to take off. *Yeeee-hah!*

Chapter Five

You know what the best part was? Woody took us back to Andy's room with him. When Andy got home, he sure was surprised to see me and Bullseye. But you know what? He liked us!

Now, Bullseye and I are happy members of the toys that belong in Andy's room. Gee, Woody sure was right—it's awfully nice to be a toy who is loved. What kind of toy would want to be in a glass case in a museum, doing nothing all day? Not me, that's for sure!